Snowboy 1, 2, 3

For Andrea

Henry Holt and Company, LLC
Publishers since 1866
175 Fifth Avenue
New York, New York 10010
mackids.com

Library of Congress Cataloging-in-Publication Data
Wahman, Joe.
Snowboy 1, 2, 3 / by Joe Wahman ; illustrations by Wendy Wahman.
p.   cm.
Summary: Illustrations and simple rhymes celebrate the wonders of winter,
from one snowboy, to ten party favors, and back to the solitary snowboy again.
ISBN 978-0-8050-8732-1 (hc)
[1. Stories in rhyme. 2. Winter—Fiction. 3. Snow—Fiction. 4. Counting.]
I. Wahman, Wendy, ill. II. Title. III. Title: Snow boy 1, 2, 3.
IV. Title: Snowboy one, two, three.
PZ8.3.W1343Sno 2012   [E]—dc23   2011034307

First Edition—2012 / Designed by April Ward
The artist used Adobe® Photoshop®
to create the illustrations for this book.

Printed in China by South China Printing Co. Ltd.,
Dongguan City, Guangdong Province

1 3 5 7 9 10 8 6 4 2

Snowboy 1, 2, 3

Written by
Joe Wahman

Illustrations by
Wendy Wahman

Henry Holt and Company
NEW YORK

1

One snowboy all alone.

2

Two children unaware.

3

Three ancient apple trees.

4

Four apples in the air.

5

Five rocks across
the river.

6

Six hills of fallen snow.

7

Seven sleigh bells softly ringing.

8

Eight mittens
in a row.

Nine pretty paper lanterns
swing from threads
that spiders spun.

10

Ten tasty party favors.

Nine rabbits
eat and run.

8

Eight points, perfect antlers.

7

Seven ruffled ravens sing.

CAW
CAW

6

Six shadows growing longer.

5

Five bears awaiting spring.

Four fish beneath the ice.

3

Three smiles
made of stone.

2

Two children now returning.

1

One snowboy all alone.